Rumpelstiltskin

1

HELEN CRESSWELL

STEPHEN PLAYER

Hodder
Children's
Books

A division of Hodder Headline Limited

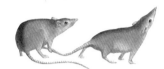

First published as this edition in Great Britain in 1998
by Macdonald Young Books

Text first published in *At the Stroke of Midnight* by William Collins in 1971

This edition published in 2004 by Hodder Children's Books
a division of Hodder Headline Limited
338 Euston Road London NW1 3BH

Text copyright © Helen Cresswell 1971
Illustrations copyright © Stephen Player 1998

British Library Cataloguing in Publication Data
A catalogue record of this book is available from the British Library.

ISBN 0 340 87787 1(PB)

10 9 8 7 6 5 4 3 2 1

Printed in Hong Kong

Once upon a time there lived a poor miller who had a very beautiful daughter. One day this man had to go and speak with the King.

He dressed in his best clothes but still he felt even poorer and humbler than usual as he walked through the high palace gates.

So when he was face to face with the King, to make himself seem even more important and a man of the world, he told the King in an offhand way,

'I have a daughter who can spin straw into gold!'

The King was very interested indeed to hear this.

'Well, Miller,' said he, 'that is something I have never heard of before. Bring your daughter to the palace tomorrow, and we will see what she can do.'

The miller could have bitten out his tongue. Why ever had he told such a ridiculous tale? For, of course, his daughter could not spin straw into gold. If she had been able, he himself would not have been living in a tumbledown mill with idle sails.

When he went home he told his daughter
what had happened, and the poor girl
wondered whatever her fate would be when
the truth was discovered? But next day she
put a brave face upon it, and she too dressed
in her best clothes and went to the palace.

The King greeted her kindly and then took her to a room that was filled with straw. The only other things in the room were a spinning wheel and stool.

'Now you can get to work,' he told her. 'And if by morning you have not turned all the straw into gold, then you must die.'

The door closed and the key turned in the lock. The miller's daughter stared round at the tumbled yellow straw and heartily wished herself safe back home at the draughty mill. She knew that she could sit there for a year, let alone a night, and still the straw would be nothing but straw. At last, because there was nothing to do but wait for the morning when she must die, the miller's daughter began to weep.

After a time the door opened, and in came a strange little brown-faced man.

'Good-day,' said he, doffing his cap, 'Why are you crying miller's daughter?'

'Because I must spin this straw into gold before morning, or else I shall die!'

'What will you give me if I spin the straw?' asked the queer little man. He was wrinkled and bearded and no higher than her knee.

'I would give you anything in the world!'
she cried, 'But I have only my necklace!'

He nodded sharply and held out his hand.

'That will do,' he said. The miller's
daughter gave him the necklace and he seated
himself at the spinning wheel and *whirr,*
whirr, whirr – three turns and the reel was
full of gold thread. He put another in, and
whirr, whirr, whirr – that was full too.

All night long the miller's daughter
watched till she was dizzy, seeing the long
yellow straws magically spun into the finest
gold thread. When the last reel was filled, the
little man bowed and doffed his cap and was
gone without a word.

At break of day the King himself came in, and when he found the straw gone and the reels filled with spun gold he was beside himself with delight and wonder. But the sight of so much treasure made him more greedy than ever, and instead of rewarding the miller's daughter, he took her to another, even larger, room filled with straw, and commanded her to spin it into gold by morning or else die.

Again the miller's daughter sat and wept and again the door opened and the strange mannikin appeared.

'What will you give me this time if I do the work?' he asked her.

'The very last thing I have in the world now,' she replied. 'My ring.'

She took it from her finger and gave it to him, and the little man sat down straightaway to spin. By morning the task was done and he went away just before the King himself came in.

The King was again delighted, and later that day he took the miller's daughter to a third room, still larger than the others. But this time he said to her,

'If you can spin this straw to gold by morning, you shall be my wife!'

As soon as she was left alone the little man appeared and, as before, asked, 'What will you give me if I spin the straw this time?'

'Alas!' she cried, 'I have nothing left to give you!'

'If I do spin the straw,' said he, 'then you will become queen. Promise me that if you do, you will give me your first child!'

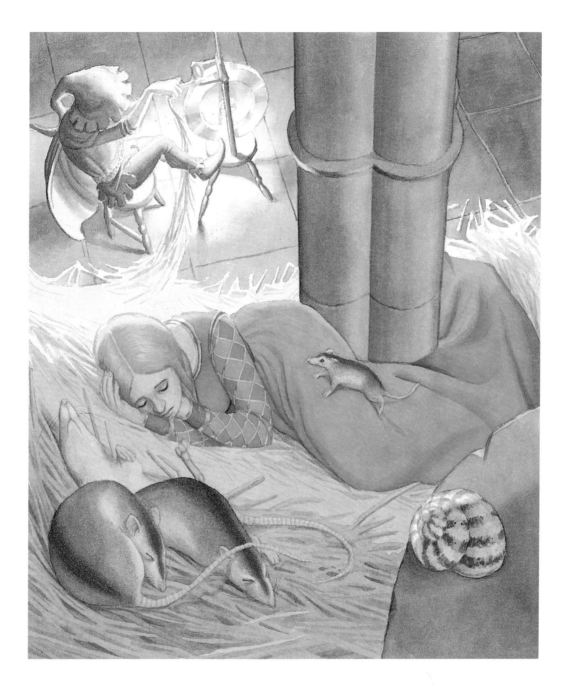

The miller's daughter was forced to agree,
and because she had spent two sleepless nights,
fell asleep to the soft humming of the wheel.

When she awoke it was dawn and the room gleamed with a faint golden light. As she rubbed her eyes and stared at the stacks of glittering gold the King entered and saw that the work was done.

'Now you shall become my queen,' he told her, 'and never more spin straw to gold.'

For he had enough treasure now to last him for the rest of his days.

And so they married and lived happily together for a year, when the queen had a beautiful child. By now she had quite forgotten her promise to the little man. But one day he suddenly appeared before her as she sat embroidering, and said,

'Now you must give me what you promised!'

The Queen was horrified, and offered him all the riches of her kingdom if he would only leave her the child. Sharply he shook his head.

'What are riches to me?' he said. 'I can spin gold from straw. But something that is living is dearer to me than all the treasures in the world!'

The Queen, broken-hearted, began to cry. The little man stood and frowned and fidgeted, and at last he said gruffly,

'Very well. I will give you three days' time.

If by then you can find out my name, then
I will let you keep your child, and trouble
you no more.'

With these words he left, and straightaway the Queen summoned a messenger and sent him out to find the names of all the people living in the neighbourhood. When the little man came back next day, she read out a whole list of names to him.

'Roderick?'

'No.'

'Caspar?'

'No.'

'Benjamin?'

'No.'

And so on right down the list.

Next day, the Queen sent out another messenger and this time gave orders that he was to find out as many odd and unusual names as he could. When the little man appeared before her for the second time, she began her list. None of the names were very likely ones – but then he was not a very likely little man, either.

'Perhaps your name is Sheepshanks or Needlenob or Lippetylegs?' she began.

The mannikin shook his head till his beard swung. The Queen went on with her list – Nobblenose, Pennyweather, Bullybags and Snout, but at every single name the little man shook his head. The Queen was in despair.

Then, on the third day, just before evening, a messenger came back with a strange tale.

'I was riding in the woods,' he told her, 'when I came to a small hut in a clearing. A fire was burning outside the house, and round it capered the queerest little fellow I ever set eyes on. And as he danced, he was shouting this song,

> '*Merrily the feast I'll make,*
> *Today I'll brew, tomorrow bake.*
> *Merrily I'll dance and sing*
> *Tomorrow will a stranger bring.*
> *Little does my lady dream*
> *Rumpelstiltskin is my name!*'

When she heard this the Queen was overjoyed. When the little man came, his eyes glowing as he looked at the baby in his cradle, she began by asking quite ordinary names. At each of them he shook his head and his eyes glittered the more.

Then, at last, the Queen drew a deep
breath and asked,
'Can Rumpelstiltskin be your name?'
The little man let out a scream of fury.

'A witch has told you that! A witch has told you that!' he screamed, and he stamped his right foot so hard that it went right down through the floor! He had to get hold of it and pull and tug with both hands to get it

out again, and when it did come out he fell right over, and the Queen and her court rocked with laughter. Then he went hobbling off as best he could, and Rumpelstiltskin was never heard of again.

Other stories to collect and treasure:

GOLDILOCKS AND THE THREE BEARS

Penelope Lively   Debi Gliori

JACK AND THE BEANSTALK

Josephine Poole   Paul Hess

LITTLE RED RIDING HOOD

Sam McBratney   Emma Chichester Clark